Level 4.8
Interest (MG4-8)
0.5pts.

Friendships in Nature

by James Gary Hines II
artwork by Jan Martin McGuire

NorthWord Press
Minnetonka, Minnesota

NorthWord Press
5900 Green Oak Dr
Minnetonka, MN 55343
1-800-328-3895

Designed by Russell S. Kuepper
Edited by Judy Gitenstein

Library of Congress Cataloging-in-Publication Data

Hines, James Gary
    Friendships in Nature / by James Gary Hines II ; illustrations
    by Jan Martin McGuire.
        p. cm.
    ISBN 1-55971-791-2
    1. Symbiosis--Juvenile literature. [1. Symbiosis. 2. Ecology.
    3. Animals--Habits and behavior.] I. McGuire, Jan Martin.
    II. Title

QH548 .H56 2001
577.8'5--dc21   2001028247

Printed in Singapore

10 9 8 7 6 5 4 3 2 1

This book is dedicated to the kids in our life:

Our daughter,
Teal McGuire,
whose smile lights up our life

To our young nieces and nephews,
Brandee and Bailey, Lauren, and Aubree,
who are the future

And to Craig and Ryan,
Welcome additions to our family

In nature, different kinds of animals help each other.

The friendships can be surprising and fun.

One animal can be very big and the other one very small.

A small animal can get into places a big animal can't.

One friend looks out for the other.

A stronger animal helps a weaker one.

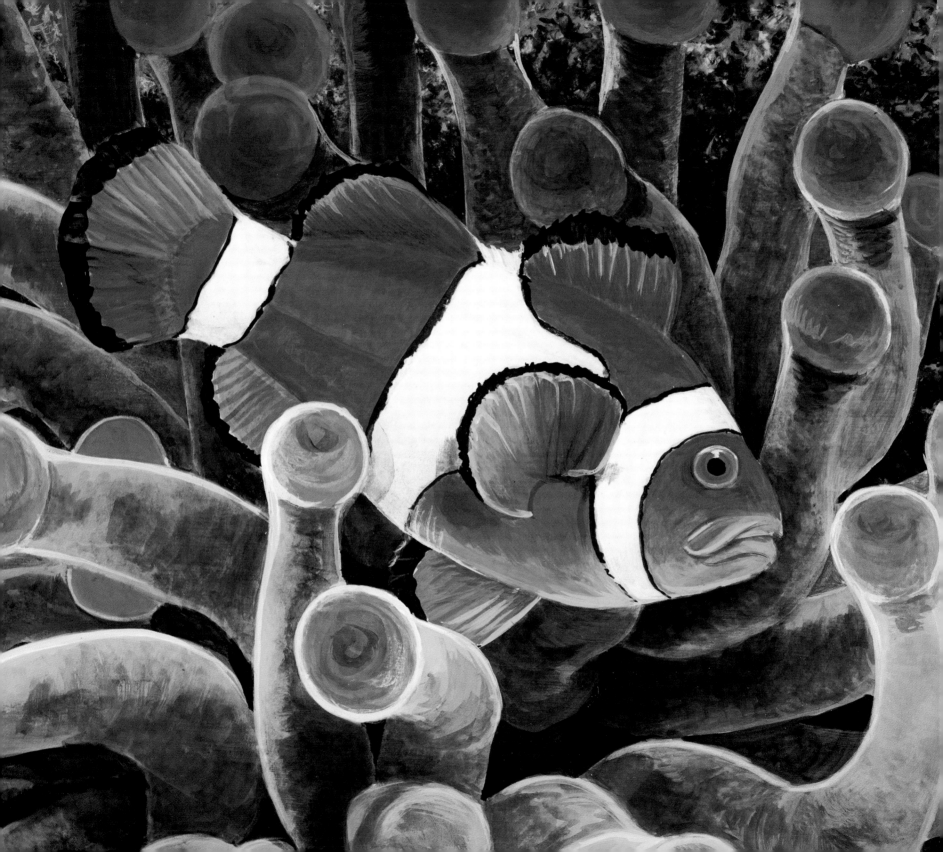

Underwater creatures help each other too.

Sometimes a plant and an animal help each other.

Insects and plants help each other.

Birds help flowers grow.

Flowers give birds food to eat.

Trees and squirrels need each other.

Sometimes animals help each other get rid of unwanted pests.

Not all animals get along
but when they do,
things can work beautifully.

The special relationship in which different species help each other is called symbiosis. Symbiosis takes place everywhere on earth and between every possible species of animals, insects, and plants.

This book shows just a few of the many different types of symbiotic relationships. These "friends in nature" work together, help each other, and make each other's lives easier.

The tall giraffe has a very long neck and very long legs. In the hot sun of Africa, many insects bother the giraffe. It is difficult for the giraffe to shoo them away. The oxpecker is a bird that spends its days picking through the fur of other animals, eating insects and keeping the animal's skin clean. The oxpecker loves the same insects that bother the giraffe. In this painting, two different kinds of oxpeckers help out a giraffe.

In Africa the crocodile and a type of bird called the wagtail help each other. After the crocodile finishes his dinner he lays on the riverbank with his mouth wide open so that the wagtail can fly in and clean his teeth. The crocodile is patient while the bird hops from one tooth to the next, collecting its dinner. The crocodile gets a free trip to the dentist and the wagtail has a free meal!

On the savannas (plains) of Africa large white birds called cattle egrets peck at the ground around animals' feet to find bugs to eat that are kicked up when elephants and other animals walk around. In return they alert animals to danger. When they see predators in the distance they call out a warning.

In the wooded areas of Africa the thick-skinned ratel, an animal that is like a badger, spends much of its time searching for honey, one of its favorite foods. The Honey Guide Bird knows where to find honey, but it cannot get inside the trees that have the beehives. The Honey Guide calls out to the ratel to get its attention. Then the Honey Guide flies low in the trees and leads the ratel to the beehive. The ratel uses its strong claws to make an opening in the tree near the beehive. He and the bird share the delicious honey and watch out for stinging bees!

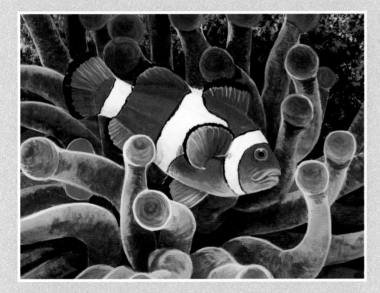

Sea anemones look like beautiful flowers with long, waving petals, but they are really creatures that live attached to the ocean floor. Because they can't move they must catch their food by using their tentacles to sting whatever swims by. Unable to move or pick up after themselves they have created a wonderful friendship with the clownfish. The clownfish is a brightly colored fish that lives among the anemones. The clownfish cleans up around the anemones by eating bits of food. In return anemones protect the clownfish from bigger animals by hiding its friend among its stinging tentacles.

The colorful Amazonian poison-dart frog lives high above the rain forest floor of Central and South America. This tiny frog lives its whole life high up in the rain forest canopy inside large, tough plants called bromeliads. The leaves of the bromeliad form cups that hold rainwater. The poison-dart frog lays her eggs and raises her tadpoles inside the bromeliad, never needing to come down to the ground. It feeds on all the bugs that might come to eat the leaves of the bromeliad, thus protecting its home.

Bull Horn Acacia Trees grow quickly in their rain forest habitat. They have sharp and strong thorns on their branches to protect their tender leaves. Sometimes the thorns are not enough to keep animals away. Acacia ants live in the hollow thorns of the trees. If an enemy comes near, the ants swarm like a tiny army and drive the unwanted visitors away. They also act like gardeners, cutting away weeds and plants that grow on or near the tree. Besides giving the ants a cozy home, the acacia provides leaf sap for the ants to eat.

Hummingbirds are sometimes called flying jewels because they come in a rainbow of colors. They can fly backward and forward and even upside-down. Their long bills are used to find their favorite food, the sweet nectar of blooming flowers. As they go from flower to flower, hummingbirds pick up pollen on their feathers. When the powdery pollen is spread from one flower to another, the flower makes seeds to grow new plants, and hummingbirds will always have plenty of nectar.

The mighty oak tree drops small nuts called acorns on the ground in the autumn. The acorns are a favorite food of the squirrel. It gathers the acorns for its winter food and buries them to hide them from other animals. Sometimes the squirrel forgets where it has buried some of the acorns. These acorns start to grow in the ground and become young saplings. They grow into tall and strong oak trees and start dropping their own acorns. These too will feed the squirrels.

This painting shows two colobus monkeys. Because they are from the same species, this is not a true symbiotic relationship, though it is an example of a very helpful friendship. Fleas, ticks and other insects burrow into the fur of the colobus monkey and bite them. The monkeys help each other get the pests off, and they get to have a tasty snack as well.

There are two species of oxpecker. One species helps the giraffe, and one species eats insects that bother the zebra. This painting shows one of the three species of zebras. This zebra has a beautiful and distinctive pattern of stripes.

Jan Martin McGuire has been painting wildlife art full time for over twenty years. Known as a naturalist as well as an artist, she travels the world over studying nature's great bounty. Her work has hung in the Smithsonian, London's Natural History Museum, Forbes Gallery, and the Gilcrease Art Museum.

James Gary Hines II has had an interest in writing all his life and has always been fascinated by the outdoors. He enjoys traveling with Jan, exploring our natural world, and helping take reference photographs for her. He handles all the business aspects of Jan's career.

Jan and James are married and they live with a wide menagerie of animals in the Osage Hills of Oklahoma, along with Jan's teenage daughter, Teal.